*To my boys,*
*may you never get*
*too old to snuggle*
*with your mama.*

This book Belongs

to

.............................................................................

***As I carry you to bed,***
***your tiny fingers***
***hold me tight,***
***I hardly want***
***to say goodnight.***

Twinkle twi
little sta

*So we sit and rock*
*in the darkness of night,*
*with just the slightest*
*slivers of moonlight.*

Twinkle,
Little
Do You
Loved You

*As you lay your sweet head on my shoulder and cling on, we rock, babble, sing, and giggle.*

***You nestle a bit closer to me, as your body starts to twitch and wiggle.***

You Are My Sunshine

*As you fall asleep,*
*your tiny fingers*
*start to lose grip,*
*while I stare down*
*at the outline of your*
*sweet cheeks and pouty lips.*

You Are My Sunshine

*It's time to lay you down,*
*but now I'm the one*
*who holds on tight,*
*as I know one day*
*I'll long for this night.*

Twinkle, Twin
Little Star,
Do You Know
Loved You

After I give you one last
squeeze and hug,
I lay you down and whisper,
"Goodnight, my sweet
little snuggle bug."

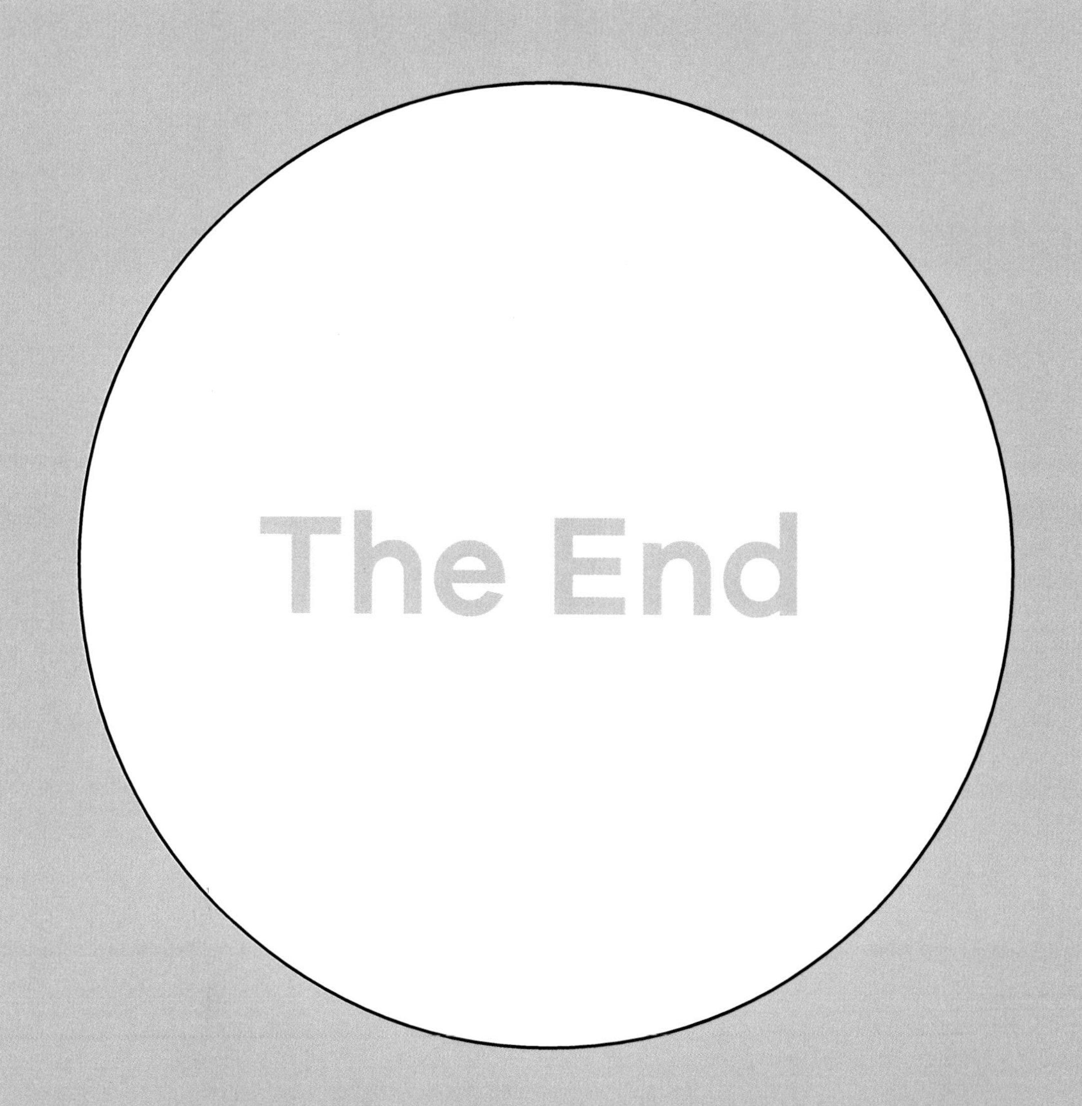
The End

# Notes

# Notes

Made in United States
Orlando, FL
12 September 2022